FIRST AMERICAN EDITION

First published in Great Britain
by Walker Books Ltd., London

Library of Congress Catalog Card Number 86-047556
ISBN 0-87113-093-9

PRINTED IN ITALY

A Bad Start
for Santa

by
Sarah Hayes

Illustrated by
Jamie Charteris

The Atlantic Monthly Press
BOSTON   NEW YORK

Santa woke up late.
He looked out the window.
It was snowing.
It was always snowing.

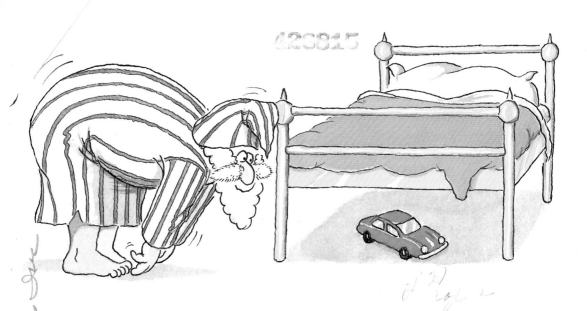

"Christmas Eve today," said Santa.
He jumped out of bed and touched his toes.
Under his bed he could see a toy car.

"Someone might like that," he said, and he
put the car into his spare sack.

He went into the
bathroom to wash his face
and brush his teeth.

When he pulled back
the shower curtain, he
was surprised to find a
large drum.

"My elves are getting
careless," he said. He
tapped the drum with his
toothbrush and dropped
it into the sack.

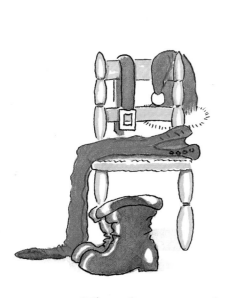

Then he put on his clothes: red underpants and undershirt; a long white shirt; a red jacket and hat trimmed with fur; and an enormous pair of red trousers.

"Now for the boots," he said. "Perhaps I ought to have new boots next year."

"I need a good breakfast today," said Santa. "It's my special day." He went into the kitchen and made himself a bite to eat.

"It's getting late," he said, and ate his breakfast very quickly. Someone had left a teddy bear in the cupboard. Santa put it in his sack.

Suddenly he remembered something.

"My mittens!" he cried. "Where are my mittens? I can't go without them."

He felt in his jacket pockets, but they weren't there. He felt in his front trouser pockets, but they weren't there either.

"Bother!" said Santa. "I'll have to search the place, and I'm late already."

He took the elevator down to the workshop.

"Have you seen my mittens?" he asked the elf who worked the elevator.

"No, S.C.," said the elf, "but I did find something in the elevator yesterday." He held out a windup mouse. Santa dropped the mouse into his sack.

In the workshop the elves were busy.

Santa had to shout.

"I can't find my mittens!" he roared.
But the elves were too busy to pay any
attention to him. And they were too busy
to see a small doll by the elevator.

"You look lost," said Santa, and he
put the doll gently into the sack.

The next place to visit was the paintshop. Santa knocked on the door. It opened a crack and a jet of blue paint shot past and landed on the wall.

"Sorry, S.C.," said an elf with blue hands and face. "What can we do for you?"

"I'm looking for my mittens," said Santa. "They're red."

"I know that," said the elf. "They're not here," he added, "and if they were, they'd be blue now." He handed Santa a bright blue trumpet and shut the door.

"Candy factory next,"
said Santa. It was
his favorite place.
One of the elves gave him
a stick of hard candy.

"I'm too full to eat it now," he said.
"I'll put it into my sack for safekeeping."
Then he shouted above the noise,
"Has anyone seen my mittens?"
But no one answered.

Santa was getting worried.

"I might have left my mittens in the packing room," he said. "Perhaps they've been wrapped up by mistake." When he put his nose around the door, all he could see was a mountain of paper and ribbon and sticky tape.

"Mittens?" he said hopefully. "Red mittens?" One of the elves emerged from the mountain.

"All mittens are striped this year," he said. "No
plain mittens at all. Not plain blue, not plain green,
not plain yellow—"

"And not plain red," interrupted Santa. "Oh dear."
Then he saw a bag of chocolate coins on the floor.

"That doesn't need wrapping," he said,
"and it shouldn't be on the floor."

The storeroom had boxes full of presents stacked
up to the ceiling, all neatly labeled. Santa caught
sight of something red behind one of the stacks,
but it was only a yo-yo.

"This hasn't got a label," he said to the storekeeper.

"Oh, take it away," said the storekeeper.
"I don't know what to do with it."

Santa looked at his watch.

"There's not much time left," he said.
"Where can those mittens have gone?"
Then he had an idea. He hurried along the
corridor and unbolted the boiler-room door.

He switched on the light and
went carefully down the steps.

"No mittens in here,"
said Santa after searching
for a few minutes. He
scrambled up the steps
and slipped on a
shiny whistle that
lay on the top step.

"What a place to
leave it," he said.

Now it was time to feed the reindeer.
After the boiler room the stable felt very cold.
Santa clapped his hands together to warm
them up.

"Those silly mittens!" he said. "Where can they be?"
He gave the reindeer an extra-large dinner.

"Do you know where my mittens are?" he asked.
The reindeer just munched their hay.
"Of course you don't," said Santa. He spied
a bright yellow ball on top of one of the hayracks.
"We really are very messy this year," said Santa crossly,
and he put the ball into his sack.

The last place to
look was the shed
where Santa kept his
sleigh. Two elves
were polishing
the paintwork.

"All ready, S.C.?" they asked.
"Not at all," said Santa. He was beginning
to panic. "I can't find my mittens. And if I
can't find my mittens, I can't drive my sleigh.
And if I can't drive my sleigh, there won't
be any Christmas!"

The elves gasped.
One of them jumped
into the sleigh.
   "Perhaps they're down
behind the seat," he said.
"There's something here."

   "What is it? Let me see!" shouted Santa.
The elf held up a painted fan.
"Oh," sighed Santa. He put the fan
into his sack and walked
slowly back to the house.
The sack was getting
very heavy.

Santa slumped down in an armchair in the hall.
He felt miserable.

"Next year we shall have to be more organized,"
he said. "If there *is* a next year," he added gloomily.
Just then a group of elves came rushing up.

"We're the counters," said one group. "And we're the checkers," said the other. "And we're one sack short!" they all shouted together. "We haven't got enough presents to go around."

"And I can't drive the sleigh because I can't find my mittens," said Santa.

"Your mittens are in your back pockets, S.C.,"
said one of the counters, "where you always
put them." Santa stood up. He felt in
one back pocket, and there was one
red mitten. He felt in his other
pocket, and there was a
second red mitten.

"You have solved my problem," he said, "and I think
I can solve yours. Is this what you are looking for?"
The elves all spoke at once. "How did you . . . ?
Where on earth . . . ? Where did you find them?"

"Oh, here and there," said Santa.
"In the bedroom, in the bathroom,
in the kitchen, in the elevator,
in the workshop, in the paintshop,

in the candy factory, in the packing room,
in the storeroom, in the boiler room, in the
stable, in the shed . . ."

"And in the hall," cried one of the elves, holding up a toy boat he had found under Santa's chair.

"And now," said Santa, "I really must be off.
One minute to go." He picked up the sack,
put on his big red mittens, and went outside.

The snow had stopped.
"It's going to be a fine night after all,"
said Santa as he waved good-bye.
"Merry Christmas!"